CONCRETE

ISLAND

Carnivale Chronicles

Anita Davis

Concrete Island

ISBN-13: 978-1-946721-15-0

ACKNOWLEDGMENTS

To my girls, Sherelle, Midnight, Trease, Gabrielle, and Ty for giving me the invaluable feedback you did during my crunch time.

Thank you so much J.L. Campbell for helping me in the last hour with keeping true to how Jamaicans talk. You are so appreciated.

Readers, I hope you all enjoy this one!

Prologue

2 Years Earlier

"Earth to Starr."

"What?" I blinked my eyes a few times, focusing my vision on one of my best friends, Rikia, who was still waving her almond-colored hand in front of me.

"So you haven't heard anything she's said for the past two minutes?" My other best friend, Tamara, chimed in right before she got back to downing what was apparently the resort's most famous drink, a rum and banana mix.

"I'm sorry, I guess I was lost in my thoughts. Everything on this island screams Bob Marley. Not in a bad way though. You can just tell how much they still love and respect him."

"Okay, Professor Night. I better not find out your fall semester freshman course is on how Bob

Marley impacted Jamaican culture," Rikia joked.

"It won't, Professor Patterson." I chuckled as I looked at Rikia. "You know, although my courses discuss the African diaspora, they primarily focus on the black experience in America."

"Yeah, they treat him like a national treasure here, but that's not it. What else had you so quiet? It's like, without moving your lips, you were talking to that lady over there that looks like you." She pointed to a resort worker not too far from us. "Just a strange stare off contest between you too," Rikia said.

Tamara sat up from her lounge chair and lifted her floppy sun hat from covering her eyes. "I knew I wasn't tripping. Y'all do favor each other a lot, and it's like she's been following us around these past three days we've been here."

"She does work here guys," I said in a feeble attempt to lessen the weight of what they were saying because I had been feeling that same way.

"Do you know her?" Rikia asked me before all of our eyes traveled over to the thick, dark-skinned woman.

Tamara's neck snapped back at me. "Sand. The woman is mopping sand. It's plain to see that something ain't right about her. If she looks over here again, you gon' check her or you want me to?"

"Down tiger. Thanks, friend, but she seems harmless, and honestly, I should've approached her day one. Something just feels different about her."

"I imagine many serial murder victims thought something was 'different' about their killer right before they snatched them up."

"You watch too much ID Channel." I eyed Tamara as she lifted her hands in surrender before pulling her hat back down over her face and reclining her full-figured body against her chaise.

I was up from my seat and halfway past the table when Rikia grabbed my wrist and said, "Hey, where are you going?"

"To talk to that lady."

"I'll go with you."

"No, I'm okay," I said the words but could see that given Rikia's raised eyebrow, she still feared me going over to the woman. I wanted my bestie to be at ease so I said, "Besides, she's not that far away. If anything happens, we'll just be a sprint away from you. She looks harmless though." I shrugged.

"Alright now, I'm right here if you need me. And Tamara will quit soaking up the sun long enough to help out too if need be," Rikia warned.

I looked back to see Tamara nod at me, and I silently thanked God for concerned friends.

I didn't know what would lay ahead when I spoke to the woman, but I needed to make sense of the eerie feeling I had in her presence. I stepped up from the sandy beach and onto the tiled deck that she was now mopping. "Excuse me?"

She stared at me for what seemed like hours before her glossy eyes blinked, and she finally said, "Yes?" in a shaky voice.

"I hope this doesn't come out wrong and I know you work here, but I've seen you more times than I've seen any other resort worker since I've been here. You seem to stare at me a lot. Is everything okay?"

The woman took a deep breath and held her eyes closed a bit before she opened and trained them back on me. "Sorry for staring at yuh, is just dat…yuh look just like mi bredda, mi twin bredda."

Things just kept getting weird for me because the woman had the same slanted but deep-set eyes like mine. Her saying I looked like her twin brother did something to me. Lost in the moment, I said, "Coincidence I suppose." I shrugged. "I guess it's true that everyone has a twin."

"Yeah, but wha' 'bout dis?" She pointed to my exposed shoulder, which caused me to slap my own skin thinking that she was warning me about a bug.

"Dere was no bug on yuh. I was pointin' to dis." She touched my birthmark, causing me to look down at her finger. Her skin was the same complexion as mine. She kept her finger on my giraffe shaped birthmark for a bit. "My twin and I have dat same birt'mark, too. In di same place." The woman pushed her uniform top off her shoulder, causing me to see my unique birthmark on the skin just below her bra strap.

My mouth was still slightly agape when the woman turned to look back at me and said, "An unusual one, right?"

"Um, yeah." My mouth went dry as thoughts rushed my brain. I had never seen anyone with my exact birthmark in the exact location as mine. And there she was saying that there was a third person with our peculiarity.

"So that's why you've been staring at me? You saw my birthmark and you say I resemble your brother?"

"And me," she whispered. "Mi just can't escape di odd feeling mi have about yuh since mi see you di first time."

"So what, you think I could be your brother's daughter or something?"

"Mi don't know. Is it possible?" Full of emotions, she held herself.

I was at a loss for words. I didn't know what to make of what the woman was saying. Truth was, I never knew my father or even who he was.

My mother was going through a promiscuous phase when she conceived me. A mixture of shame and not wanting to own up to her ways caused my mother to not even pursue finding out who my dad was.

The sordid look of emotions on the woman's face pulled me from my musings. I shook my head at the surrealness of it all.

My girls and I had only come to the island to unwind and enjoy ourselves, but the woman's suspicion and inquiry had shifted my world in a matter of moments. "You know…I'm sorry…what is your name?" Not being lost on manners, just in the moment, I held out my hand to shake hers.

"Zeporah. What's yuhs?" Her thick accent was so beautiful.

"That's such a pretty name. I'm Starr." She held my hand longer than a normal handshake would be with a stranger and it caused me to look down at our joined hands. There was something so homey about the way she gripped my hand.

"Starr. Starr." She repeated my name as if she was in awe of it and was trying to commit it to her memory. "Starr, yuh such a pretty young gyal."

"Much like yourself, right?"

She chuckled. "I didn't want to say it, but yuh is di spitting image of me when mi was younger."

"I bet." I finally pulled my hand from hers, reeling in the fact that I looked more like her than I did my own mother. "Zeporah, to answer your earlier question, I've never known my father, so I don't know who he could be or where he could be from. What you're alluding to could be plausible, but I hate to say, more than likely, it's way off base."

Her features saddened and her countenance pierced my heart.

"Mi get it. Me t'inking that yuh could be mi brother's daughter may be off base, but mi just can't shake dis feeling in mi gut." She paused for a second and then said, "Mi wish mi could have mi phone on me during work, because yuh could see how much you two really look alike." She looked defeated for a second, but then she said, "Mi get off at four. If yuh meet mi out back, mi can show you some pictures."

Staring at her, one of my brows immediately lifted.

"I get your worry, but mi really want yuh to see what mi talkin' about."

"I-I don't know."

"Okay. If you don' show up, mi won' bother you another day you're here. But if yuh just as curious about me and mi brother now as I am about your connection to us, then you'll be out back at four." Her face lit up with hope and then she walked away.

The attentive stares of Rikia and Tamara rushed me back over to the table and I shared with them my encounter with Zeporah.

"Starr, I am not letting you go back there to meet that woman. This has scam all over it. She'll get you back there, kidnap you and be expecting us to pay the ransom to get you back."

"Again, you watch too much ID channel," I admonished Tamara.

"She does, but she's right, Starr. This sounds like a scam." Rikia patted my hand.

"I know it sounds crazy, but we look so much alike guys. We have the exact same birthmark in the exact same location on our bodies. And when she squeezed my hand…it just felt different…familiar."

That familiarity, curiosity of what Zeporah had said to me is what had me sandwiched between Rikia and Tamara as we stood in the staff quarters of the resort waiting on Zeporah.

"Starr." Her voice caused me to jump and my friends to draw nearer to me. "Sorry for scaring yuh. Mi just happy yuh come to meet mi here." Clutching her purse suspended from her forearm, she came to stand in front of me. "I hadn't been able to focus on anything the rest of the day, wondering if you would come out here. Hello." She nodded and smiled at Tamara and Rikia.

"Hi," they said almost in unison.

She looked at me for a while, a longing in her eyes before she finally pulled out her phone, fidgeted with it, and then handed it to me.

I barely had the phone up in my face before shock settled in the bottom of my stomach.

"Yuh can go right and see more pictures of him," Zeporah directed me.

I heard her but couldn't get my thumb to move on the screen. If the pic of what I would look like as a handsome man wasn't enough to floor me, any others might bury me from the disbelief I was in.

I couldn't move and was grateful for my friends planking and propping me up, but Tamara wasn't against scrolling through more pics of Zeporah's brother. Five pics later and the usually chatty Tamara was just as silent as I was. A quick glance at her caused me to see wide eyes and a gaping mouth. Her shock matched mine.

Rikia must've been the most composed between us because she cleared her throat and said, "Starr, I don't think this is a scam. Perhaps a very odd coincidence, but even I can't deny how this woman would assume you're her brother's child."

"Can you take me to him? We can talk to him together and I can see if he's ever been to Chicago and if he ever came across my mother."

Zeporah pinched her lips together. "Mi wish mi coulda do dat, Starr, but him dead ten years ago. Mi miss him dearly ever since. We did close, especially after we parents dead. We did only have each other, but after dat him dead inna boating accident.

"When mi see yuh dat first day, mi start to have hope. Like what if, even though mi brother lef mi, him lef a piece of himself here and mi just find it."

She looked deep into my eyes and I choked up. There was so much despair in her voice. I wanted to be her niece to comfort her…and to finally find out about a part of me I felt like had always been missing. "What was his name?"

"William Brown." The corners of her mouth

slightly lifted.

"Zeporah, how about I take down all of your information, give you all of mine, and I'll get in touch with you once I get back home and talk to my mother?"

"Mi woulda like dat." She reached in and pulled me into her embrace.

1

Starr

"It ain't Trinidad and Tobago, but this bomb Carnivale you helped spearhead will be in full swing two weekends from now. I can't wait to show off my belly ring and scantily dressed size sixteen body down on Northerly Island." Tamara swung her butt length weave over her shoulder and shimmied in her seat.

"Okay thicker than a snicker," Rikia said to Tamara. Tamara often referred to herself as such so we all laughed as we sat around the table in Rikia's office. It always seemed to be our meeting place whenever Tamara stopped by campus to see us in between showing houses to her real estate clients.

"Starr?" Tamara looked directly at me. "You

know anything about how many people plan to attend Carnivale? Any celebrities coming into the Chi to soca with us? And by celebrities, I mean fine melanated men ready to come in and shimmy in nothing but some shorts and sweat covering their sculpted bodies."

"So you haven't seen the flyer, the performer's lineup?" I asked with a bit of shock in my voice.

Tamara frowned, marring her otherwise gorgeous face and fell back in her seat. "I mean yeah, I have, but the only superstar I saw on it was JoJo's old stuck up ass."

"Leave her alone." I waved Tamara off. "She is mad talented."

"I didn't say she wasn't. She can sing. I'm just saying, I ain't checking for her. Wrong gender," Tamara quipped.

My shoulders slumped. "You just heightened one of my worries. Not enough people in Chicago know about Carnivale. I need as many of us," I rubbed my skin to point out its dark hue, "to come out. Not only for the optics, but to learn more about our rich cultures and to celebrate us in all of our glory."

"Ooo wee, ever since we got back from Jamaica two years ago and you showed your momma that pic of your daddy and her kitty-kat remembered he indeed was the one who knocked her up, you have been so…Jamaican."

Rikia buckled over in laughter while I chided Tamara's antics. "First off, don't ever bring up my momma's lady parts again. And secondly, I'm proud to know I'm part Jamaican."

Holding her stomach, Rikia calmed her laughing down long enough to look at Tamara and say, "Wait, please tell me the story again. I hate that I was not there to experience Ms. Night's response for myself."

"I can't stand either of you heffas." I adjusted in the armed chair in Rikia's office, knowing that there was nothing I could do to stop Tamara from jumping up and retelling the story for what had to be the thousandth time.

Her tiny waist very much so contrasted with how wide her hips were. She had killer curves and knew for a fact that her measurements had been the undoing of several men. She adjusted her pencil skirt on her slim waist and said, "Okay, and you know I ain't lying because I tell it the same every time just like it happened the first time."

Rikia chuckled.

Tamara positioned her cinnamon-colored hands in front of her as if she were waiting for a football pass as she prepped to tell the story. Her theatrics would be in full swing. "We settled in Ms. Night's kitchen and Starr wasted no time in recounting everything that happened with Zeporah in Jamaica. Baby, when Starr walked over to her mother and held up her phone, Ms. Night gripped her countertop. And not like because she had seen a ghost, but it was the look of a woman who vividly remembered a man knocking the bottom out of her thang."

"You make me sick," I shouted at Tamara.

She chuckled. "I'm sorry Starr for putting your momma on blast, but you know I ain't lyin'. She literally started fanning herself, and you helped her to sit down thinking she was merely distraught, but then the next words that came out of her mouth let us know she was everything but."

"What she say, girl?" Rikia asked, a grin plastering her face.

"Girl, she said that she conceived Starr, and I quote 'during her hoe phase'. She said that she particularly had a craving for dark men at the time and couldn't have separated them from one another if her life depended on it. But when Starr showed her that picture, it all came flooding back to her senses. Ms. Night said she had never had a man do her like he did, and the memories were why her lower extremities were beyond her control as she stared at the pic of him.

"She said he was the best that she ever had, and it stood to reason why Starr looked just like him. She said he put it on her so that she could only succumb to the way he handled her body. Said that he did *all* of the work that night, made her see stars, and was probably why she named the product of that night,

Starr. She looked at Starr and then at his picture, fanned herself, and said, "Job well done."

That last part always sent Rikia into a laughing fit that had her wheezing and Tamara well pleased with her reenactment skills.

I needed their laughter at my expense to be over with so I said, "Enough already. I hate hearing about my momma and my daddy's sexcapades."

Tamara finally rejoined her seat at the conference table we sat at and said, "Girl, that moment will never *not* be funny to me, so deal with it. But look at it like this, your momma's memory of him comforted you to do the blood test with Zeporah and confirm that she is indeed your aunt and that William was your father."

I could only smile recounting the past two years of getting to know my aunt. "Yeah, she's fast become like a second mother to me. She's taught me so much about my Jamaican heritage, which is why I'm glad everything came together with the city approving the Carnivale.

"Immersing myself in the culture, I familiarized myself with the places that Jamaicans frequent here and it's clear to see that we need even more representation in this melting pot, this concrete island of mine. This Carnivale is gonna bring the tradition and richness of the carnivals of the Caribbean and South America to Chicago. I just need to get folks to show up and learn about the Afro-

Caribbean folks that live here and abroad."

2

Chris

"Brothers and sisters, we have a problem." Judging from the wide-eyed stares and eerie silence in the room, my opening statement to those in attendance at the mid-week "town" meeting had made just the impact I'd wanted it to.

I needed their undivided attention. The black population of the city of Chicago needed their undivided attention.

"We are dying." I knew my words were raw and unfiltered, but they were real.

"You ain't lying. My neighbor's sixteen-year-old son was gunned down just last week."

I held my hands up in the air to ward off any other testimonials. "I'm sorry to hear that Mrs.

Rutledge, and while those stories are rampant and sad across the city, I'm not talking about us literally dying. I'm talking about the black population in Chicago is dying." I looked to see a few shoulders relax, some head nods and pursed lips mix in with the attentive stares of those around me.

"Chicago, which once boasted the third largest black population in the states has fallen. We are experiencing a reverse migration. Many of your parents and grandparents came here to escape Jim Crow practices in the south and to take part in the booming steel and meat plants thriving in cities in the Midwest.

"Because I have extensively studied our history here, I know that there went from being 40,000 of us at one point to 180,000 within a couple of years. Of course, those numbers continued to grow over the decades and put us at one million in 2000. But guess what the stats were for us the last time they did a soft census."

"50!" Mrs. Rutledge's five-year-old grandson called out and garnered a few laughs across the room.

"Hush, boy and play that game." She popped his hand before crossing her arms again against her plump middle and then looked back up at me.

I couldn't help but grin at his estimation. At least he'd been paying enough attention to know that his number should've be lower than the one I had said. "Not that low, DeMarcus." I rubbed my low and scruffy beard and briefly paced the front of the room before I stopped and looked at them. "Guys, we were numbered at a little under 800,000 in just 2017. Now tell me that ain't a crime."

"It ain't! The crime is all of this senseless killing going on. Rutledge talked about her neighbor's son being killed, but I've had a thirty-year-old son, a ten-year-old niece, and a sixty-year-old cousin all killed by gun violence in the last three years. I'm sick of it. If I could, I would leave here too." Mr. Kelly lamented and was followed by the chatter of several others around the room sharing their losses with those nearby them.

I gave them a second to share their grief with their elbow partners before I called the meeting in the storefront alderman's office back to attention. "Hello. Excuse me. Ladies and gentlemen, what I'm saying here is in no way meant to overshadow or diminish the loss you all have experienced due to senseless violence. I just want to take the time tonight to point out a big issue that is occurring for us in our hometown. Mr. Kelly, if it weren't for the violence, would you still want to live in Chicago?"

Before he could even speak up, Kesha, a thirty-year-old, stood up and said, "I know that question wasn't directed at me, but I have something to say. I haven't experienced losing a loved one, but there is nothing here for me. I was born and raised here, went away to school at Mississippi State and came back home wanting to start my career and family here, yet neither have been possible for me for the past seven years."

"But you're college-educated, you should be able to get a job in your field here," Mrs. Rutledge turned and blurted out at Kesha.

"Exactly." Kesha slapped her hands against her slim hips.

Mrs. Rutledge snapped her head back to look at me. "Christopher, aren't you single?"

I was caught off guard by her question, but I answered her truthfully. "Yes, ma'am. I am."

She turned and looked at Kesha again. "Kesha, you just said that you want to start a family and you'll need a man to do that. Why don't you two hook up?" She pointed at Kesha and then at me. "I mean, look at Christopher, he's tall enough, dark, and a very handsome young man. He's always in shape since he's a personal trainer too. His hair is too wild for my liking, not like the neat, big afros we used to wear in the 70s, but he always looks groomed. He's educated. Got a degree in black studies." She shifted in her seat and I could hear her mumble, "I didn't know one needed to study how to be black, but that's besides the point."

I chuckled a little but didn't bother to interrupt her. She did this every year with trying to hook me up with one of the women my age that came to the meetings. Things never worked out with the women though. They weren't much into social change and barely made it through three weekly meetings before I never saw them again.

Mrs. Rutledge got back on her spiel. "You two could make some cute and smart babies. You might even have fun in the process." She turned back to face me, crossed her hands over her fluffy waist, and smiled at me like her interruption was witty and hadn't thrown off the important topic at hand.

I was eager to redirect the audience, but I couldn't help but to take in a blushing Kesha. I had to admit that she was cute with her long braids, fit physique, small stud in her nose, full lips, and bold round eyes, but I was more concerned about my activism in Chicago than settling down with a woman.

Plus, I couldn't just get with any woman. Many spent more time taking digs at me for being "woke" rather than following after the latest fashion trends and being abreast on all things pop culture. A lot of the women in the neighborhood didn't even look my way because I didn't wear skinny jeans, grab my crotch every chance I could, or call them out of their names as some twisted sign of affection.

After a brief and hopefully subtle perusal of her physical features, my eyes landed on hers and I inwardly cursed at Mrs. Rutledge's suggestion because there Kesha was, staring at me all googly-eyed and a small smile perching her lips. She was giving off that vibe that she would take me and Mrs. Rutledge up on the offer if I gave it to her.

I had to get things back on track. "People, people, we need to bring the meeting back to its intended purpose. While you all cite the violence in the city as the main reason you want to leave, the reality is, it's not as bad as you think it is. Given our population, Chicago is like number twenty-one of twenty-five in rankings of the most violent cities on many lists."

Eyes bulged after I stated those facts.

"That can't be true," an attendee said.

"But it is and you wanna know why?" I scanned the crowd and found them all focusing on me.

"Yup," DeMarcus shouted and nodded but never took his eyes off his game.

I could only laugh at his intermittent attentiveness and hoped that by his grandmother always bringing him to neighborhood things, it would spark a fire in him to be an agent of change in the future.

"Believe it or not, DeMarcus' contributions to our conversation aren't a distraction for me."

Mrs. Rutledge harrumphed.

"They're reminding me of what's really at stake here and why I need you all onboard in this fight with me. The crime is not as rampant as we think it is here. That's just the narrative the media allows to rotate. Again, anyone know why that is?"

"Don't give me a conspiracy theory, Christopher," Mr. Kelly shot at me.

"It's not, sir. I have data to back up everything I'm saying to you all. They—"

"Who is this 'they' you're talking about?" Mr. Kelly asked. He was known to be stubborn and argumentative, no matter the subject matter. If you commented on how blue and clear the sky was, he would point to the faintest grey cloud and say, "It ain't that clear out here."

"Don't play dumb, Roy. You know the 'they' he's referring to. Whitey," Mrs. Rutledge said the last of her words through pursed lips.

Mr. Kelly looked up at me as if to confirm what Mrs. Rutledge had said.

"Well yes, whites hold a lot of power in this city, but it's not just them, it's equally about those with money that dictate and govern how things go in this city. Wu-Tang said it best, C.R.E.A.M."

Many of the older people in the room eyebrows furrowed, but I smiled at the ones in my age range as they nodded at me. They understood me. "I'm just saying that cash rules everything around us. That and false senses of superiority.. They are driving us out with the sensationalism that Chicago is too violent, and we need to flee it. Meanwhile, they come in our neighborhoods that they wouldn't live in with us, buy the houses dirt cheap, and then when enough of us have left, they move in and create beautiful neighborhoods."

"But violence isn't the only issue plaguing Chicago, jobs are scarce here too," Kesha offered.

"You're right, the jobs that many of our sisters and brothers are qualified and legal to work are scarce, but there are other fields, jobs, and opportunities abundant here."

"Like what?" Kesha cocked her head to the side.

"Check this out, how many black-owned beauty supply stores are there in this neighborhood?" I asked.

No one answered.

"Right, none. And yet the Asians have cornered that market. We are the number one customers, yet we don't think to supply the demand. You wanna know why? Because by the time many of us get to the age where we wanna do something like own a business or get a high paying job, we have felonies and misdemeanors that prohibit us from getting the small business loans and even the start-up grants that they get to open a business.

"They have always done everything they can to oppress us. I don't know why they want to push us out of such a freezing cold place, but that's their objective. We have to rally together, weaponize ourselves with the appropriate knowledge and resources to stop this forceful exodus of us from Chicago. Brothers and sisters, we have to act now."

"Act how? What can we do to get *us* to see that things aren't as bad as they seem in Chicago and not to just up and move?" Kesha said with such passion in her voice that I couldn't help but to stare at her a bit longer than I should have I guess. She had me looking at her differently just that quickly with her attentiveness to what I had been sharing.

I pulled my thoughts away from her to address what she had asked, what others may have been thinking as well. "Guys, we have to educate ourselves and the generations coming under us about our history, disenfranchisement, the fact that we belong here just as much as the next race.

"We have to go down to City Hall and tell them we know what they are doing and demand that they create more jobs for us, provide more funding for our schools, rather than investing millions into the rebuilding of neighborhoods once we've fled them. We have to make them invest in us and our neighborhoods now."

Mostly everyone in the room, except for Mr. Kelly, who was putting his hat on and walking towards the door, gave me their undivided attention. They soon were caught up in the detailed and more visual plans I shared with them via a PowerPoint presentation.

Kesha even moved up to the front row and I appreciated her enthusiasm as I divulged what I had come up with thus far.

3

Starr

"Rikia, I'm just not pleased with the amount of RSVP's we've gotten on social media." I walked into her office at the university without so much as a call or text to let her know I'd be showing up there. I figured it be okay given that I knew that she didn't have another class until three pm that day. I used my best friend privileges and showed up unannounced.

She didn't even bother to look up from grading papers when she said, "Girl, people are gonna show up."

"But how can you guarantee they will if it doesn't have the visibility I think that it should?" I took the seat in front of her desk, grabbed the bag of open, mixed nuts and poured myself a handful before

I rejoined my seat.

"Starr, I can't guarantee it. You just have to have faith. But if you're that pressed about it, do more to make it stand out." She sipped water from a bottle nearby and replaced it on her desk without making eye contact with me.

Her lack of looking at me didn't bother me since I had infringed on her time. I knew that she was dedicated to grading during work hours and taking as little work home with her as possible.

Me on the other hand, I didn't mind grading papers at home. But grading schedules was not why I was there, so I leaned forward in my chair and said, "Do more?" My elevated voice warranted the eyebrow lifting stare she shot at me. I knew I was on edge so I quickly said, "Sorry for snapping on you."

"It's cool. I'll give you a little latitude on the matter since it's something you value so much." She gave me her full attention with those words.

"Thanks. I just feel like everything I can do within my power and my natural resources has been done, but it's not enough. I need help."

"What about the planners you gave the idea over to, isn't marketing it their department?"

"Yeah, I check in with her and her company from time to time. They try to assure me that it'll be a great turnout, but I don't hear the buzz that she claims the streets have."

"Maybe that's because you don't be in the

streets." Rikia laughed and pushed her big and naturally loose curls behind her ear. She wore her hair big and untamed just like mine. But hers went past her shoulders while mine was cropped above my shoulders.

"Whaddya mean gyal? Mi out and about all de time. You know I've become a regular at Kingston on Friday nights and Reggie's Lounge on Saturday nights."

"First off, didn't we talk about you and that broken patois of yours." Rikia couldn't keep a straight face before her shoulders bounced as she chuckled.

"The only way I'll learn it is if I practice it. You better hush before I go visit my aunt for a whole summer again to practice it and miss your birthday celebration. I'll definitely get better at it then."

"Miss my all-white party this year if you want to."

The razor-sharp glare Rikia cut my way let me know she wasn't playing. I squeezed her hand, stopping her from grabbing her pen to get back to grading papers. "I was kidding, friend. I wouldn't miss your party for the world. But seriously, you know my goal, so help me."

"I honestly don't know how I can help you besides the old school way of hitting the pavement with some flyers...but, I know of a guy who's actively involved in his community and known around town. He may be able to help you get the word out."

I smile wide but then frowned at her before I said, "So why didn't you tell me about him the first time I brought this up to you?"

"Because I didn't think of him then, but better late than never."

"You're right."

"I know." She laughed, causing me to purse my lips at her. "We went to high school together. He's great with organizing people, drawing attention to his causes, and community outreach. I'll text you his info."

"Thanks."

"Is that all you need?" She barely looked up from the stack of papers on her desk.

"Yes, because I'm certain that with the minimal amount of attention you've been giving me, you wouldn't dare stop to help me plan my presentation to share with the crowd for the opening of the weekend."

"Hey, you came in on my planning period. I love you, but you know that I like to take care of business during business hours."

"I know." I grinned. "I'll leave you be, for now, but thanks for the connect with the guy."

"You're welcome. And close the door after you." Rikia laughed as she looked up at me.

"Goodbye, darling." I left my friend's office

excited for the connection she would hopefully helped me make.

I was just excited for what was to come.

4

Chris

"It's so good to see so many returning faces as well as new ones." I couldn't help but to steal another glance at the deep brown-skinned beauty with the wild fro like mine, sitting at the back of the room. I had never seen her before, but my eyes were well pleased with her presence. "Mrs. Rutledge, DeMarcus, even you, Mr. Kelly and the rest of you all who came back a second time this week for a discussion lets me know that you got what I was saying the last time we were here."

Mr. Kelly grunted.

"You all coming back tonight means you're willing to journey with me."

"I'm just here for the donuts and orange juice," Joe, the neighborhood homeless man, shouted from the refreshment table.

"That's okay Joe, you keep coming and you'll learn something. Maybe even enough to change your situation," Kesha offered.

"From what, fit to fat eating these donuts? Because otherwise, ain't nothing wrong with the way I live." Joe snipped.

Most of the neighborhood residents knew not to argue with Joe about his living conditions. Countless winters and summers of trying to get him checked into shelters proved that we could only offer him food and a few coins every now and then.

"It's alright Joe, eat as many donuts as you want." I looked back at the crowd in front of me. "As I was saying on Tuesday, we're experiencing us leaving Chicago in big numbers and for reasons that should not be the case." I wanted to keep my focus on the points that I was about to dole out, but I couldn't help but to sneak peeks at the newcomer. She seemed to be so in tune with what I was saying, and I hadn't even begun my spiel.

I was a leg man and it was summertime in the Chi. She had come in rocking denim shorts that fell mid-thigh and a flowy orange spaghetti strap shirt. I didn't make a habit of ogling women, out of respect of them being more than just eye candy, but her meaty thighs and the gloss she wore on her full, soft-looking lips kept my eyes busy stealing glances of her. And her untamed hair, big and in its natural glory? A win in my book.

There was something about a black woman rocking her natural hair, free and loose that touched my soul. As if it were her unspoken declaration that she was unashamed of her heritage.

I pulled my thoughts from her and back to my meeting thoughts. "How many of you all have experienced family members, friends, colleagues leaving this great city for what they consider better opportunities and living elsewhere in places like Atlanta, Dallas, and Houston? To name a few."

Majority of the room lifted their hands.

"Because of what some are calling and I see for myself, strategic gentrification, we're fleeing in droves."

"Strategic gentrification?" Mr. Kelly shouted.

I knew that if he showed up, he would be one I would have to be thorough yet concise with my explanations. "Yes, Mr. Kelly, it's when improvements are made to a neighborhood above what the current residents can afford. It's an attempt to push them out and make the neighborhood more suitable for middle class and above social classes."

To that response, I got a hard headshake from him before he said, "Sounds like you're saying that the city is driving us out."

"Yes, that's what I'm getting at."

He waved me off and then stood. "No one else is our problem. We are our own problem. The 'man' didn't shoot my son. A man that looked much like him did. We are killing ourselves, hurting our ownselves."

"Mr. Kelly, it's not that simple. A lot of our behaviors result from systemic oppression and issues we as blacks have been facing since we touched down, unwillingly, in this country."

"I see you're one of the fools that thinks what happened over four hundred years ago still has any bearing on us. Just dumb." He shook his head as if he pitied me.

"Roy." Mrs. Rutledge shifted quickly in her seat to face Mr. Kelly. "Don't be all up in here calling this young man dumb. He's smart, obviously smarter than you. Now, if you don't like what he's saying, you can leave. But I won't let you stand there and continue to insult him. Got something negative to say, direct it to me and see how far you'll get with calling me dumb."

Mr. Kelly chuckled as he turned to look at Mrs. Rutledge. "Rutledge, I ain't scared of you. I'd be to the door by the time you lifted from that not so sturdy seat of yours."

"Roy." Mrs. Rutledge rocked back and forth trying to get up out of her seat, but the silent beauty's voice from in the back rose above the ongoing chatter stirring the crowd.

"He's right." She stood. "Gentrification is happening in a lot of the neighborhoods in Chicago. Look at what type of buildings and businesses have popped up near the United Center since the Henry Horner Homes were torn down. Those businesses wouldn't dare have rooted themselves around there when those projects were there. Believe him or not, you can look at an apartment finder online and see how much a one-bedroom is priced in those neighborhoods. The area is no longer meant for those that once lived in those projects. He really is speaking the truth." Smiling at me, she took her seat just as quickly as she had stood from it to come to my defense.

I can't even lie, she had more of my attention than she had from just the exceptional sight of her.

No sooner than the nameless beauty sat down did Kesha jump up from her seat on the first row. "Yeah. Christopher is absolutely right."

The way she said my name caught me off guard a little. It dripped from her mouth like it was the sweetest thing she'd ever said and there were those googly eyes of hers again staring at me. Instead of directing her attention to the rest of the audience, she kept them trained on me like I was her prey and she continued speaking. "Everything he's saying is right."

We waited for her to say more, but she only

continued to stand and just stare at me. I wasn't sure of it, but her coming into the alderman's office every day after she got off work to "pick my brain" on my activism raised a concern for me. With the way she had been saying my name, always trying to be close to me, I realized that the "couple" seed that Mrs. Rutledge had planted in her had blossomed into a plausible reality for her in such a short time. I was going to have to figure out a way to let her down without hurting her feelings.

"Thanks, Kesha." I nodded at her, which must've given her clearance to sit down again because she did so. I put my attention back on my stream of thought before others joined in and led us away from the meeting's agenda. "You'll hear some people argue that it isn't really gentrification since our low-income neighborhoods aren't technically being replaced by whites but are just riddled with a lot of abandoned buildings.

"The reality is, they won't admit to what's really going on. If we let them carry on as they have, we'll look up one day to see that they all have touched down and set up residence in our neighborhoods and that none of us are no longer here.

"It's true that they haven't replaced us yet in many of the desolate neighborhoods. But that's because there are still too many of us living in them for their liking. They are eagerly buying up the vacant lots, foreclosed homes and businesses, and biding their time before they settle.

"Minimal funding is occurring in *our* schools and community resources and all that matters to us in a strategic effort to move us out. Make no mistake that our mass exodus from Chicago is not just a coincidence. It is the strategic placements of policies and manipulative and repulsive practices enacted by city officials to push us out."

Kesha smiled at me as if I were Dr. Martin Luther King and had just closed his infamous "I Have A Dream" speech. She looked at me with such pride in her eyes that I thanked God I was getting ready to bring the meeting to a close and would put some distance between her and me.

"There's so much else I want to and will share with you all, but I know I can't give it to you all at once. No one gets all of the nutrients they need at once. But rather when they eat balanced and nutritious meals all throughout a day do they properly feed and fuel their bodies. I've been feeding you with what I've been saying and these pamphlets that I'm about to pass out will be more nutrients. It's fuel that will build you up and help you fight this fight with me.

"We have to march, rally, pass out flyers, disrupt city hall with our presence and voices, support black businesses and less and less of theirs to get them to see that we see what they're doing, that we mean business, and won't be pushed out of this great city." I held my fist up in the air because I honestly took pride in what I was saying. I took pride in us. "More of my thoughts and initial plans are in the pamphlets. Please read them as soon as possible. Let's fight back."

No sooner than the last of my words had left my mouth did Kesha rush to me and take the pamphlets from my hand and began to pass them out.

"Thank you." I nodded at her.

She blushed and walked away on her mission.

I knew I had to keep the meetings short and measure out my thoughts to them, eating too much at one time was rarely ever good. I thought I had given them more than enough to digest during the meeting and hoped they would be fired up and even come back with suggestions of their own the next time we met.

"People, please eat the rest of the donuts and juice." I shook a few hands and said goodbyes to some of the residents mingling around the room before the deep brown-skinned goddess who had captured my attention during most of the meeting worked her way to me as I made my way to her.

"Hello, I'm Christopher Combs. And you are?" I extended my arm to shake her hand.

"Starr. Starr Night."

Her smile was bright, her eyes so deep and alluring, and her hands so soft that I didn't want to let it go. I wanted to keep hold of her hand and simply gaze at her, but her smile widened, and she slipped her hand from mine.

"I see you're as powerful up close as your words and presence are from a distance."

I tilted my head a little. "Starr, are you macking me?"

Her head fell back a bit and she didn't hesitate to laugh loudly.

"I'm serious." She had me blushing like I was in fifth grade and she was my first crush. The distance between us during the meeting hadn't afforded me the up-close opportunity to take her in.

She wasn't that much shorter than my five-ten stature, a plus for me because I wanted a woman to be my equal in many ways. She had these adorably cute and puffy cheeks and her eyelashes were so long. Made me want to stare in her eyes for an eternity, but she had finally composed herself from her laughter.

"No. I'm not macking you, just honest and upfront enough to tell you that you speak with such conviction and are knowledgeable about the topic at hand. I can't help but to deem you powerful and an agent of change. Present and future."

I covered my hand with my chest and swayed a little, showing her I was taken by what she had said. "I don't care what you say, you're trying to talk me out of my cargo pants."

"You are silly." She giggled and lightly punched me in my arm with the comfort and ease of a person who had known me all of my life. "That is not why I'm here."

"Good, I wouldn't let you take advantage of me like that so soon anyway. You'd at least have to take me on a date first."

Grinning, she shook her head. "Christopher, I came here because I was told you might be able to help me."

I couldn't help but to take on a more serious demeanor with her declaration. I was ready to assist her in any way I could, especially if she was a business or a homeowner and someone was trying to push her out of either all in the name of gentrification.

Yeah, I didn't know her situation but had already plotted her problem. I guess that's because I was interested in her and my head was already formulating a way to help her.

"Get out of that head of yours. You're scowling, but my dilemma isn't that bad. It's not a life or death matter."

I felt the tension ease in my face at her admission. It was crazy to me how I was so invested in this woman within such a short amount of time. I was all ears with Starr and wanted to give her my undivided attention but couldn't help but to notice a matter out the corner of my left eye. Kesha lingered nearby, straightening chairs that were already perfectly aligned with one another.

I put my attention back on pretty Ms. Starr.

"Chris, can I call you Chris?"

"Call me whatever you'd like." I winked.

"Chris…" She grinned. "To make a long story short, I campaigned to get the city to approve a Carnivale to be held down on Northerly Island to celebrate the Afro-Caribbeans in Chicago and our culture. Like I said, the Carnivale will celebrate but also educate and enlighten the residents of Chicago of the rich history of Africans dropped off in the Caribbean during the slave trade."

Her demeanor dampened a bit with the last of her words and I could only imagine why. What she had last referenced had been an unnecessary and tragic occurrence for our ancestors.

"Wow, I've seen flyers around town and on social media for the Carnivale, but I never would've imagined that someone as beautiful as you would've been the brainchild behind it."

She smiled again, blushed actually and I was glad that I had lifted her mood again.

"Thank you. I didn't do it alone. I had the help of a lot of great people who saw my vision for what it was. But I've grown kind of nervous that not enough people know about it. In sharing my worry with my best friend, another professor over at DePaul University, she suggested that I come see if you could assist me. I need help getting the word out more about the Carnivale. She figured you were the best man for the job since you're very active in the community, visible and vocal about our issues."

I paused a bit, mulling over my thoughts, looking to choose my words carefully because I didn't want to alter the vibe I felt between us, but I just had to be me and honest in response to her request. "Starr... Forgive me for being so blunt, but I can't rally behind your cause when I'm working tirelessly trying to get mine in the spotlight."

She pursed her lips and her forehead scrunched.

"There is a greater work to be done in Chicago beyond pumping up what out of touch pop star will be on a stage for a weekend," I added.

She put distance between us by taking a step back.

"But, but..." I wanted to get to know her more, so I rushed to say, "You can join forces with me. Residents of Chicago or anywhere on the globe for that matter can read about our rich and sordid history of the diaspora at any time, but if we don't act now on this exodus, we won't be able to afford to move back in once we've all left. Our forced departure from Chicago is where all of *our* attention should be."

She took a deep breath and looked to summon a fake, tight smile on her face as she simply said, "Have a good day, Christopher."

She walked away before I could get another word in. Our impasse of what was really important for our people seemed to ruin the moment between us. Her sudden departure irked me.

Why couldn't we have met under different circumstances?

5

Starr

"So, how did it go the other day with that community activist I told you about? You refused to talk about it when I stopped by your office the next day," Rikia asked as she stirred vanilla creamer in her coffee as we sat in the fairly empty café not too far from campus.

I hope my poked-out lips conveyed my feelings about the meeting because I really didn't want to talk about it.

"And no, your sour face isn't an answer enough for me. Spill the beans, Starr."

I slowly pulled my tangerine tea bag from my mug, placed it on the stack of napkins nearby, and carefully folded it into them in an attempt to avoid responding to her inquiry.

"Starr!"

"Okay. Okay." I moaned. "In no way shape form or fashion did the convo turn out the way I thought it would. In addition to me thinking that I would've left out of the meeting with an ally to help promote Carnivale, I thought I would have left with us exchanging numbers. Why didn't you tell me that he was so fine? So engaging?"

"Because, I didn't know that would be relevant to what you're trying to accomplish," Rikia said casually.

"Um, ma'am, best friend, let's not act brand new with each other. No matter the cause, you should always inform me of whether or not a man is fine before I meet him. I'm talking about it looked like he put lotion on every day."

"What?" Rikia laughed.

"No, really. His skin looked so firm and not just from all of the muscles I could see from his broad shoulders to his meticulously sculpted calf muscles, but his deep, rich skin looked supple like he was into self-care."

"Alrighty then." She lowered her head and rubbed her forehead like she was in disbelief of my assessment of him.

"The defined curls in his big fro looked soft, his teeth were so white and pretty, his cute, Nubian nose, tantalizing dark brown eyes and his voice? It was deep and passionate. He commanded my attention with it." I was so lost in recounting his looks but then a thought jumped out at me. "Wait, did you plan to keep him for yourself? If that's the case, I'll renounce my attraction to him and cast it into the sea of forgetfulness."

Deep creases were visible in her scrunched forehead. Rikia looked at me long and hard before she said, "I wasn't looking to keep him for myself. And I'm glad you were attracted to him. It's been a minute since you've had a constant guy in your life."

"As we discuss all of the time, it's not that I don't want a man, I just haven't found one that suits me. Until then, I'll dabble here and there from time to time. And no need to worry, he won't fit the bill to be a constant. He pretty much scoffed at my plight."

"Come on, it, he wasn't that bad, was he?" She propped one of her elbows on the table and rested her chin in her hand.

"Let's just say that the attraction bubbling between us fizzled down to water by the time I walked out of there."

"But water is still powerful." Rikia laughed.

"Whatever. It sucks. After you told me about him, I had really gotten my hopes up that Mr. Activism would be down to help me promote the Carnivale."

I didn't make a habit of sulking, but I couldn't help but to slump a little in my seat. "I mean, given his passionate talk of saving the black population in Chicago and how we were being disenfranchised in many facets, I just knew he would've been on board when I made mention of the diaspora. No matter where we ended up, we've all had our struggles and yet have beautiful traditions and ways of life that deserve to be highlighted and celebrated."

"You're right," Rikia offered me what I knew was heartfelt sympathy.

I sat up and squared my shoulders. "While my attempt to team up with Chris to get the word out didn't pan out, my resolve to make the Chi-Flavor Afro-Caribbean Carnivale its best is unyielding. I'm proud to have found out about my Jamaican roots, even if I was twenty-nine when I did so. As I've told you countless times before over the past few years—"

Rikia nodded and I grinned at her.

"Whatever." I playfully rolled my eyes at her. "The Jamaican, Caribbean community for that matter is so vibrant and tight in the city and yet we don't get the support and visibility we rightfully deserve. I'm proud of everything Auntie Zeporah has shared with me about my dad, my culture, and I want to share it with everyone I can. So back to the street, passing out flyers on my own it is."

"Or, you can make it apart of your students' grades that they have to help you pass out flyers and share the weekend on their social media."

"You're silly. Although an interesting idea, you know I can't do that," I said.

"Excuse me, ladies."

I turned to see where the soft voice had come from and jumped a little at the sight of who it was. "OMG, you're Val Warner, co-host of Windy City Live."

"I'm certain she knows who she is," Rikia whispered.

Val laughed. "Indeed, I am. Ladies, I didn't mean to, but I couldn't help but overhear you alls conversation. Starr, is it?" She pointed towards me.

"Yes."

"I've heard about the Carnivale you mentioned and a little bit of how it came to be. I'd love for you to come on the show tomorrow and talk about it."

I could feel my eyes bulging out of their sockets and my heart racing fast. I couldn't believe what she had just said.

"You speak with such passion about the matter. I hate for you to feel defeated, so if you're willing to, I'd love for you to share your journey in discovering your Jamaican roots. Although I don't know the story in full, it seems like one worth broadcasting and getting wrapped up in. You can also use your time on there to promote the Carnivale. Hopefully, you being there would create more exposure for the event."

"I would definitely be open about my journey. Just tell me what time and where to be. And thank you so much for this opportunity." I stood up and reached to shake her hand.

She gave me a firm shake and said, "You're welcome." She reached in her purse, pulled out her phone, handed it to me and said, "Plug your number in there. A programmer from the show should be calling you within the hour. Take care, ladies. I look forward to seeing you tomorrow, Starr."

"Same here, Val. Thank you so much." I sat back down so full of nervous excitement. She left the mellow café and I turned a bright smile back to Rikia.

"See. Where there's a will, there's a way." Rikia smiled.

"Yes, there is!" I shouted softly before delighting in my then room temperature tangerine tea.

***

"Studio audience, let's welcome our next guest, Professor of African and Black Diaspora Studies at DePaul University, Starr Night."

Prompted by a man running across the front of them, the audience clapped loudly and I thanked the heavens that I didn't have to walk out into the palpable energy in the room. I wasn't a klutz, but given how nervous I was to be live on a national show, there was no telling if I would've made it to my seat without having stumbled or my knees giving out from all of the giddy nerves racing through my body.

"Thank you all for having me here." I smiled wide, not being able not to show all of my teeth. I waved at the audience first and then nodded at Val and her co-host, Ryan Chiaverini.

"Guys, I so happened to be in a café last night and overheard Starr speaking with so much passion about what she's going to talk about with us today. I promise you all I was not trying to eavesdrop," Val chippered.

"Yeah, right," Ryan chimed in.

The audience was cued to laugh, and they followed suit.

"Really. But I'm glad that I did catch the parts of their conversation that I did. It sounded like a plan for her endeavors had fallen through. She sounded defeated at one point and I knew I was in a position to help her, so I made a call to move some things around for today's show and voila! We have this beauty here to share her story with us."

"I guess your eavesdropping benefitted the talker this time around," Ryan said.

"Yes, it did." I felt the need to speak up.

"So Starr, dive right in and tell us about your story and this magical Carnivale I can't wait to go to."

"My pleasure. Again, thank you all for having me here. This opportunity is amazing. I'll briefly share my recent history, which I feel helps to explain why I was so passionate about getting the Carnivale approved and recognized by the city and not just some random fest offered during the summer.

"I didn't grow up with my father. I didn't even know who he was, but after an odd yet fulfilling girls' trip to Jamaica, I found out who my father was from his twin sister at that."

Ryan's eyes widened.

"I know, right. I wish I could tell this story bit by bit, but I know that's not possible at the moment. Once a DNA test confirmed William Brown was indeed my father, there I was with the newfound knowledge that I was half Jamaican. The revelation didn't make me abandon my pride as a black woman, but rather doubled it to know that I had Afro-Caribbean roots as well. Many visits and time spent with my dad's sister, Auntie Zeporah, in Jamaica afforded me a close-up, firsthand look at how rich and storied Jamaican culture and traditions are, is."

"I bet," Val chimed in.

"Missing Jamaica when I'm not there, I sought out the Jamaican community in Chicago. It's beautiful and tight-knit. And so are other black islanders. Just being immersed in it all made me want to expose all of Chicago to it rather than people only ever so often going to a reggae themed party."

"I get it. You want to see that part of you represented as much as black women want to see themselves positively highlighted in mainstream media."

"Exactly." I loved that Val, a black woman, was one of the co-hosts and got what I was saying without even saying it. "I took the idea of the Carnivale, because if you know anything about how they are celebrated in places like Trinidad and Tobago and Brazil—"

"I certainly do." Ryan smiled in a way that said he had an interesting story.

"So, you're sharing your carnival chronicle next?" Val asked, amusement dancing in her eyes.

"And get fired? I think not," Ryan answered quickly.

We all laughed.

"Sorry to cut you off. Continue, please." Ryan directed his words at me.

I smiled at him. "I wanted to bring that energy to our city with the city of Chicago officially putting their stamp of approval on it. Plans were made, people were talked to, permits were approved, and next weekend's grandeur is possible because amazing and supportive people saw my vision and helped to execute it. I just fear that not everyone knows that it will be going on next week."

Val looked to the audience. "How many of you all heard about the Carnivale before today?"

Literally, only five people raised their hands.

"While there was only a handful of people that

said yes to knowing about it, now the whole studio audience knows and everyone who tuned in live today knows. And for those of you at home watching, pay it forward and tell others about it," Ryan admonished them.

"Yes, I checked out the website and they have something to do for everyone. They're giving you carnival and Carnivale vibes. You still have time to grab some feathers and dance your way down to Northerly Island next weekend. We'll be back after this commercial," Val said, and we all began to dance in our seats as soca music filled the studio speakers.

6

Chris

"DuSable Building, where is the DuSable Building?" I mumbled the words to myself as I stood in the center of the campus. The information desk must've given me the wrong directions because I still hadn't caught sight of the building.

But maybe they weren't to blame. My frustration that led me to go there may have muddled my sense of direction. But at any rate, I was dead set on finding the building and the room that she was in.

Looking at my watch, I realized I couldn't afford to lose any more time, so I grabbed the attention of the first person nearing me. "Excuse me. Do you know where the DuSable Building is?"

"Ugh, right behind you," the young woman answered me with a perturbed look on her face before she walked away from me as if my question where absurd given my proximity to the building I was looking for.

"Thank you." I ignored her dismissive tone of voice and headed towards the DuSable Building.

After that, it didn't take me long to find the classroom since it was on a schedule at the front door.

I slowly pulled the door open, hoping to quickly take a seat since I heard her talking to her students, but she looked up towards the door and her words faltered as we locked eyes. A bit of shock covered her face before she looked back at the projector behind her to seemingly regain focus on what she had been saying.

I hesitantly pulled my eyes away from her beauty and scanned the lecture hall for a seat. I was somewhat surprised to see the room was packed. Not because she wasn't captivating with both her looks and the way she exuded confidence and commanded attention with her words, but because it was a Tuesday night class during the summer, and it was full.

In regards to some college courses, students don't show up to class. They rely on the notes from their friends, but clearly, people wanted to be in her class. Not because she was administering a test, but I gathered it was because she knew her stuff. Her delivery was engaging and evoking.

I temporarily forgot the outrage that had sent me there. I found myself nodding my head a little in agreement with her dissection of a point as I squeezed past people down a row to sit in the only empty seat available at the back of the lecture hall.

"…I'll end it with that note on Pan-Africanism."

Judging from the rustling bookbags, her telling the students what chapters to read for their next class, and the eager chattering of those nearby, things were coming to an end.

I watched her pack her messenger bag as the lecture hall emptied and she talked to the few students who had approached her. I briefly reflected on how convicted she was about the subject matter she discussed that night and how she pushed her students' critical thinking. *Was I becoming a fan of hers?*

When the room was fully empty, she made her way towards me and stopped just short of the row I endcapped.

"Christopher."

"Starr."

"What brings you here?" she asked with indifference coating her words.

"You."

"Me? How did I do that?"

"I received a call late last night saying that my segment on Windy City Live was being canceled and didn't know when and if they would reschedule me to come on."

I stared at her and thought I read a look of knowingness, but she remained quiet, so I continued. "Of course, I was flustered by the idea that I wouldn't get to talk about my cause on a platform like theirs, but imagine my frustration when I tuned into the show this morning to see that you had stolen my spot to talk about your Carnivale."

She chuckled a little and the fire in me that had doused itself after listening to how dope and magnetic she was during her lecture reignited. Unfortunately, it came out in a rather harsh tone of voice. "What's so funny?"

"Nothing funny per se, just that it's interesting that you could be so one-track minded to think that only your issues matter."

"What I'm focusing on is more pressing than your party. You know I was going to talk about voter registration and even how gentrification is spearheading the black exodus from Chicago – matters that deserve around the clock and national attention. But I was shut down from talking about them on the show because of feathers and music." I couldn't help but sound sarcastic at that point.

Her eyes narrowed. "So, did you watch the entire segment? Get the *why* the 'feathers and music' are so important to me?"

"No, I didn't get past the host saying that you worked here. I couldn't bear to watch you talk about the party when I should've been on there talking about my plight." What I refused to add to my answer was that I couldn't keep the TV on and look at her fine self up there on set glowing, much like she was in front of me at that moment.

"Seeing as though you came to my alderman's office to talk to me, I thought it was fair for me to come here and talk to you about what's really important. Why don't you use your thought-provoking prowess for real community activism rather than putting your energy and efforts on trivial things?"

Grinning, she shook her head at me. "Christopher, you don't know how I use, as you say, 'my thought-provoking prowess'. And it's unfair and frankly rude for you to say that my efforts are trivial, *especially* when you don't know the basis of them. Let me leave you with this, since you seem to be lost on the notion. As a people and given our history across the globe, we are more than capable of being passionate about and championing for more than one cause at the same time. Have a good evening, Christopher."

She walked out of the lecture hall and left me feeling some type of way again.

I hated to admit that she was right about us being able to focus on more than one cause at a time, but dammit, I needed mine to rise above all others. And that wasn't me being a narcissist or ego-trippin', that was me being really concerned about the decline of blacks in Chicago

.

7

Starr

"It's so dope that DJ Double Down just connected you with his DJ Red over at WGCI radio station. You get to go on air and promote Carnivale on his show tonight. But what I really wanna dig into is Chris coming to your class Tuesday night." Rikia's dark brown eyes widened with wonder.

"Yes, that is so nice of Double Down. And yeah, girl, Chris brought his fine and pompous tail to my lecture." I rolled my eyes. "Why does it seem like we're most often attracted to assholes?" I said above the reggaeton as I swirled the straw in my drink and leaned into talk to Tamara.

"Not sure about other quote, unquote 'assholes', but Christopher isn't one. You're just annoyed that he's as passionate about his cause as you are yours,"

Rikia chimed in.

"Whatever. All I know is that he needs to keep his dismissive energy away from me."

"Is that the only energy he gives off?" Tamara leaned into me as she winded in her seat. She was loud and what she was hinting at was loud as well.

"I can't tell. The only energy he gives off is that I'm in his way."

"Nah, there's more than that. Otherwise, you wouldn't mention him being fine as often as you do, and he wouldn't stir you the way he clearly does. When you're turned off by a man, nothing can persuade you to look at him other than like a toad," Rikia said and Tamara fell over laughing at her.

Not one to hold back with my girls, I said, "Yeah, it seemed like a good, romantic energy between us when I caught him staring at me at his meeting, and when he sat in my lecture, but our face to face convos seem to overshadow the fizzle popping between us whenever we lock eyes."

"Ooo, girl, that's my jam." Tamara plopped her empty glass on the hard-top ottoman in front of us and rushed out to the dance floor to roll her plush hips to Red Rat's "Tight Up Skirt".

I couldn't lie, it was one of my favorites and had me gyrating in my seat as Rikia and I laughed at the short man trying to keep up with Tamara's big booty bouncing to the song .

"For real though Starr, would you give him a

chance if he stepped to you like that?"

"I would. I would be a fool not to. He's fine." I chuckled knowing how many times I already mentioned how gorgeous he was to me but then I got back to sharing my thoughts with Rikia. "But beyond that, he's very smart, has a strong sense of community, motivated, and purpose-driven, but I don't think he can handle being with someone who's as passionate about her own goals as she would be about his. Not sure that he gets that he doesn't have to have a follower in a woman. We both can lead *and* take each other's leads as necessary."

"Lord, Momma Deep done came out of her bag."

I chuckled and sipped the last of my drink. "Whatever. Listen, we came to wine, grind, dutty wine and unwind tonight. Enough of talks of Christopher. This is my song and I'm about to get lost in it." I winked at her and pulled on my bodycon dress as I got up from the plush bench we sat on and swayed to the song. Soon my whole body was in sync with the midtempo, Skip Marley song.

With the bass thick and heavy, the guitar strumming my mood just right, the song held me in such a trance that I bent over as my back dipped and my shoulders and hips rolled me right into a standing position and then I locked eyes with him.

It was dark in the lounge, save the red, green, and yellow strings of light sparingly throughout the place, but still, I could see him. And clearly, he could see me because I seemed to keep his attention as much as he kept mine.

Rather than play coy with him, since that wasn't my style, I continued to wind to the music and crooked my pointer finger, beckoning him to come over to me.

Apparently, he wasn't shy either, because he forced his way through the sea of couples and singles slow winding on one another and came to stand in front of me.

I could've said something at that point, ask him what he was doing there, seeing as though I was a regular at the place and had never seen him there before, but I decided to just let the music talk for us.

Skip Marley and H.E.R.'s "Slow Down", acoustic version of the song filled the place.

The title of the song alone was necessary for him to hear. With his arms stiff at his sides, the tension I felt in his body was enough for me to play the teacher role and treat him like he was in need of a lesson.

"Relax," I leaned in and whispered in his ear as I gripped his wrists. I felt him shudder and appreciated the fact that I hadn't imagined that I was affecting him. Still winding and swaying to the music, I stared deeper and deeper into his eyes until I spun and helped to guide his hands to my waist.

Another slow winding song started that I absolutely loved to dance to. I continued to dutty wine on him and could tell he had relaxed and was giving into the experience between us since he was somewhat moving and was keeping a firm grip on my waist, keeping my butt in close contact with him.

Winding and grinding on him, I reached behind me and grabbed his neck and he rested his chin on my shoulder as we completely fell in sync with one another.

I could feel the bulge in his jeans pressing against my butt, which made me arch my back and really grind into his tight hold of me before I couldn't help but to turn around and look at him.

When I turned to face him, I kept my eyes trained on his as I winded my pelvis into his.

My face moved in closer to his and I could feel his ragged breaths painting my face. I pulled back a little from him to see the faintest smile on his face. "You should do that more."

"What?" He grazed the tip of my ear a little after he leaned in to whisper in my ear.

The action sent an exhilarating shiver down my spine and I guess my shudder caused him to rub his hand up and down my exposed arm.

Everything about our closeness, the moment, felt so right. I wanted more of it from him. "I was saying that you should loosen up more around me. It's beautiful."

He chuckled softly, but then his smile faltered a little and his voice deepened when he said, "But not as beautiful as you."

Those few words of his led us into a deep eye-fucking session as we barely swayed to the music but held on to one another.

A throat clearing behind me tried to pull my attention from staring into his eyes, but whoever was trying to get past us would just have to squeeze by, or if they were trying to cut in on our dance, they were out of luck because neither one of us seemed concerned with leaving each other's embrace, presence.

I felt a tug on my arm before the voice of the offender leaned in and said, "Starr, sorry to interrupt y'all, but if you want to get down to the station on time, we have to leave now."

I grunted and looked at Rikia over my shoulder. "Okay, I'll be there in a minute." I looked back at Chris thinking the connection that held us so closely together for the past couple of songs would have passed, but when I looked in his eyes and still saw the mixture of curiosity, admiration, want, and a few other things I couldn't quite make out, I knew that special energy was still strong between us.

Interlacing my hands with his, I leaned in and whispered in his ear, "I have to go now."

"Do you really?" His voice held so much disappointment that I wished I could stay there with him the rest of the night, but I just couldn't forfeit the opportunity I had been given to advertise the

Carnivale on the radio for free.

"Yeah," I pulled back to look in his pretty brown eyes. "I hope to see you again soon, though."

"Me too." I heard him say as I hesitantly released his hand and was rushed away by Rikia and a whining Tamara for having to leave the club at that point in time.

***

"Chicago, I'm not whispering in the dark because I have to scream this out loud."

I couldn't help but laugh at the locally famous nighttime DJ who lulled me to sleep with his slow and sexy R&B many weeknights over the years. He also had kept me amped up on weekends with his hit list of bangers blaring through my speakers when I came in from partying.

"Chicago, we have the lovely, Professor Starr Night in the building, in the studio."

His energy was infectious and made me sit more upright in my seat. I'm certain my wide smile cracked my face. I tampered it enough to talk into the mic positioned in front of me. "Thank you so much, DJ Red for having me here tonight."

"It's our pleasure. Listen folks, DJ Double Down over at Reggie's Lounge helped to get Starr in here and for a good reason, so listen up. Tell the people what's coming next weekend to our fabulous city." He motioned his hands as if he was giving me the floor to speak.

I patted the headphones on the side of my head to make sure they were secured, leaned into the mic a bit more and said, "Hi everybody, like DJ Red said, we have something big coming to Chicago next weekend. Hopefully, most of you all have heard about the Chi-Flavor Afro-Caribbean Carnivale being held over at Northerly Island, but if you haven't, you can go to www.chiflavorafrocaribbeancarnivale.com to learn more about it.

"There, you'll see that carnival games and rides will go on all weekend long, so it's family-friendly. There will be a parade Saturday morning and then the bands and dancers, playing mas', will light up the city with their festive colors and music. And we'll conclude the weekend on Sunday with some of the hottest musical acts in the world. Please share the weekend with all you know. There'll be loads of fun from a magnificent Afro-Caribbean culture that you need to experience."

"Sounds great and you know I'll be there. We have to get back to the music, but once again folks, that was Starr Night, one of the initiators of the Afro-Caribbean Carnivale going on next weekend that you and yo' momma nem need to be at."

He put on a Snoh Aalegra hit and then looked at

me and said, "Starr, it was a pleasure having you here and I hope that being on the air helped to make the crowd bigger next weekend." He stood and held his hand out for me to shake.

In return, I stood and shook his hand. "DJ Red, please know that I definitely appreciate the opportunity to promote the event on your show. I'll get out of your way and get home to listen to the rest of the show. Can you throw in some Bob Marley or Sister Nancy's "Bam Bam" in about an hour? I'll be home by then."

"Sure thing. Be safe." He smiled, sat back down and put his headphones on again as his show producer cued him for the commercial break.

I quietly stepped out of the studio, overwhelmed with giddiness that I was given yet another opportunity to promote the Carnivale. Hopefully, people who didn't know anything about it were tuned in while I was on-air and would soon be among the Carnivale attendees experiencing the vast and beautiful festival cultures of Afro-Caribbeans.

8

Chris

"We won't be pushed out!" I shouted the mantra
I had come up with on the ride over to DePaul
University's campus.

I had graduated from Howard University with a
degree in Afro-American Studies and knew how
involved my student cohorts had been in striving for
social change. With that in mind, I figured going to
Starr's school where they had a similar degree
pursuit, I could hopefully persuade the students there
to join forces with me to save *us* in the city.

Because I had shared my plans with those that
attended my weekly meetings, Kesha had
volunteered to accompany me to the campus that
evening. Although I knew her help could benefit me,
I didn't want her to confuse our time together away

70

from our headquarters as some kind of quasi-date.

Fortunately, with us being busy actually engaging most of the people we stopped on their paths to and from classes, we barely had spoken to each other during the hour we had been out there. I was grateful for all of the buffers and was ready to call it a night when I turned to face Kesha and tell her it was a wrap, but locked eyes with Starr as she crossed the center of campus.

That gravitational pull, the one that sparked between us the first time we met and came to a head when we danced, caused us to walk towards one another. When she was an arm's length from me, she spoke first, "Christopher."

"Starr." I was feeling her but not her cause and the latter must've come out in my dichotomous tone.

She chuckled, more like scoffed at me. "Why do you…hate me? I thought we remedied that with our dance the last time we saw each other."

"I don't hate you, I just…" I sighed. "I left the club after you left that night. I took a ride down Lake Shore Drive and thought I would vibe to the playlist DJ Red normally hits us with on Saturday nights, and imagine my…surprise." Since I had quickly changed my last word from what I was thinking, I offered her a tight-lipped and fake smile before I got back to talking. "I heard you on a big platform, yet again, promoting your party. I'm just frustrated with the access you're given to speak to the masses versus the platform I have. I honestly feel like your time can be better utilized talking about the effects of systemic racism, gentrification, underfunding, and so much more ailing our community than promoting your party."

"So you're pretty much a hater?"

"What? No." I couldn't bring myself to be too mad at her off assumption, given how attracted to her I was.

"It would be greatly appreciated if you would stop reducing the Afro-Caribbean Carnivale as just a party. I'm starting to think that you don't know your history, your roots."

"I do."

"I'm not just talking about the history of African Americans in this country but those of the diaspora as a whole. Because if you did, you should have better insight as to why the carnivals are so important to us abroad." She pointed at me and I felt the sting of her words and saw the fire of her conviction in her eyes.

"I—" she didn't let me utter another word before cutting me off with her finger still aimed at my chest. It was a wonder that she hadn't reached out and poked me yet.

"I've heard your plight enough times to get it, but clearly, you haven't heard mine enough to let up on me at the least, so let me spell it out for you. We are *both* about the empowerment of our people.

Obviously, I care about the social issues affecting *us*. That's why I'm an AA studies professor. I studied and became one to drive home to students the richness of our origins, help them to think critically about our history, and show them how that knowledge and urge to do something positive with the information affects the present and future generations.

"While you're walking around with your chest puffed out thinking that your voice is the only one that matters, I really want to know who made you God and gave you the authority to decide whose cause is greater and better than the next person's?" She folded her arms across her chest and stood there tapping her foot as if she were waiting on an answer to what I thought was a rhetorical question.

I'll admit that if it were any other woman standing there silently demanding for me to speak like she was, I would've wished her well and kept my distance from her. But I couldn't.

This woman had beckoned me from across a dark and crowded room with just her alluring eyes and the crook of her finger.

Her way with words and intellectual mind wooed me long before the curve and swivel of her hips had molded perfectly into the embrace of my body.

A woman who had me dancing in public when I don't do it even in private. One who had me thinking

about her when I had so much else to worry about–
she was truly something else. Her beauty and vibe
was too magnetic to ignore.

With every encounter with her, I recognized just
how layered she was. She didn't annoy me, but more
so my platform not getting the exposure and backing
I felt it needed is what vexed me.

I guess my musings had kept me silent for too
long, because she dropped her arms and said, "If you
can't come at me better the next time you see me,
with your head out of your ass, keep walking by."
With those words, she offered me the same fake
smile I had given her earlier and then she walked
away.

My eyes probably would've watched her
fleeting back until she was no longer in my view, but
Kesha walked up to me. She caused me to lose sight
of Starr when I looked back into the crowd of people,
hoping to spot her in her bright orange top that
popped against her sun-kissed and beautiful skin.

"Kesha?" The befuddled look on her face made
me say her name as more of a question.

"You know what, I'll save you the trouble of
trying to let me down in the subtle way you have
been."

"What are you talking about?" My forehead
creased.

"I mean, you don't look at me the way you look
at her. Or engage me the way you do her."

I felt like her bringing it up was a good time as any to talk about matter and yet I didn't know exactly what to say. I didn't want to offend her or hurt her feelings.

"Really, it's fine. I could see that you weren't interested in me. I mean, when Mrs. Rutledge put us on blast that day, you never approached me like you were interested in me. I should've took that as a sign, but I volunteered even more with you in an attempt to get you to see how great of a woman I am."

"Make no mistake about it, you are a great woman."

"Yeah, just not the woman for you...That wasn't a question, more like a statement of fact. Good thing that we didn't ride here together, now we don't have to have an awkward ride home." She buffered the brief silence between us with a humorless chuckle.

I sighed. "Kesha."

"Christopher, it really is okay. We miss all of the shots we don't take."

I smiled at her metaphor, thinking on how big of basketball fan she told me she was.

"And don't worry about it, I won't lessen my volunteering in an attempt to avoid you. I know that everything does and doesn't happen for a reason, but if I can offer you some advice?"

"Yeah, sure." I could only admire her for how well she was taking things not going anywhere between us. And not that I felt that she was so beholden to me that letting her down would've shattered her world, it's just that in today's time, people are more prone to having meltdowns when things didn't go there way rather than embracing noes.

"Like I said, it's plain to see that you're into her. Don't be the idiot that wants a woman but lets her get away because of his pride. I didn't hear much of what she said, but what I did hear her say was right. You both have great causes that are meant to empower blacks and can be strived for at the same time. Don't think that your cause is better than hers. Keep it up and you'll turn her off and push away someone that could be good for you and good to you."

My brows lifted at her bluntness.

"Don't be so surprised by me. I figured since you don't mince words, you would want me to shoot straight from the hip, so I did. Think about what I said and since you know she'll be at the Carnivale this weekend, maybe you should be there too. Might expose you to more people to pass these out to." She waved the pamphlets in her hand at me. "And you might even have the chance to right your wrongs with her."

"Well, tell me how you really feel, Kesha."

We both laughed.

"Come on. I'll walk you to your car." I motioned towards the concrete path that would lead us back to the parking lot.

"Thanks, but I'm okay. It's such a beautiful night. I think I might walk the grounds a bit more before I head home. Enjoy the rest of your evening."

"You too, Kesha." She walked away and I was left alone not only with my thoughts but with what Starr had said to me as well as Kesha's upfront advice.

It was a no brainer to see just how perfect Starr could be for me given her passion for us as a people, her all-around energy, and the vibe between us. But I probably had run her off with my need to push my agenda above hers.

9

Starr

"All around the world, people gather at carnivals to celebrate life. The Caribbean calls it a creative and artistic festival of expression that's exhibited through colorful parades. Chicago has gotten in on the action with our very own Chi-Flavor Afro-Caribbean Carnivale to bring some of the island flavor and heritage to the city." I stood on the mainstage for the weekend and looked out at the beautiful and big crowd, spread across the grass outside of Soldier Field, cheering loudly and I had to fight back the tears stinging my eyes. So many of us had shown up and I couldn't have been any more elated than what I was at that moment.

I took a deep breath and got back to the task at hand, delivering the opening speech that Saturday morning. "Not that my profession makes me more knowledgeable than anyone else on the subject matter, but since I am a Professor of African and Black Diaspora Studies at DePaul University, for years I have been a student of us, our origins and our legacies. I have intimate knowledge of the exceptional gifts and elevating contributions of African and African descended people, communities and countries in regards to societies here and all over the world and I'm in awe of it all.

"While most of the morning will focus on what is called 'playing mas', bands competing with the best DJs, costumes, and dancers, it is done so and with pride because for years on islands like Trinidad and Tobago, enslaved Africans weren't allowed to participate in the 'prestigious' masquerade balls called fetes. We were mocked with blackface in the festivals but were forbidden from participating in them even though they had stolen the concept from West African religious cultures and societies.

"But as always and with centuries of oppression, hatred, and ignorance spewed at us, we take derogatory things and dire situations and flip them. We reclaimed what our ancestors invented and amped it up. Emancipated slaves shortened the masquerade to 'mas' and rebooted the festival to reflect the carnivals celebrated in today's time.

"So what you'll see as 'playing mas' is not just an excuse for us to drink and dance in the streets, but it's our, descendants of the Diaspora, ongoing declaration of just how rich, inventive, and beautiful our melanin, heritage, music, and creativity is. The Afro-Caribbean community in Chicago is beautiful, you guys. Commune with your brothers and sisters today as we celebrate.

"Rejoice in knowing it is a celebration of our foundations, our ancestors. It is a celebration of life. Enjoy it all on our concrete island." The resident mas' band playing on stage amped up the music and the crowd on the grounds in front of the stage went wild as they raised their cups and began hopping and dancing to the lively music.

My heart was overjoyed by the sea of jovial melanin before me.

I danced my way offstage and headed to meet up with Rikia and Tamara to change into our mas' costumes and get dolled to play mas'.

***

Chris

Even though everyone around either had beer in their hands and was dancing to the music or adjusting their bright-colored costumes, I never passed up the chance to share my cause with a crowd of blacks in the city.

I had come armed with a messenger bag full of

pamphlets briefly outlining my plight and the ways in which we could end the exodus.

Because I believed I was built and equipped and so passionate about the lives of African Americans, I knew that once we stopped and reversed the exodus, unfortunately, another pressing issue for my community would steer me in its direction. I was okay with that.

"My brother—" My greeting to the man next to me was cut off by the dismissive wave of his hand before he ushered the crowd he was talking to away from me.

Used to people brushing me off before I even shared why I had approached them, I turned my attention to the woman heading in my direction. "Excuse me, can I talk to you for a second?"

"Sure." I could see her flirtiness dancing in her eyes.

"Are you aware of how many black Chicagoans have left the city within the last couple of years?"

"No, I'm not." She smiled at me in the salacious way most women did when I approached them. I knew I was handsome and that my muscular and lean frame unintentionally lulled them into feeling comfortable with talking to me. And while I let my exterior comfort them, I never flirted with them and gave them the false hope that I was coming on to them.

Well, that was until Starr. Even though she

didn't rally behind my cause the way I wanted her to, everything about her still called out to me in a way no other woman ever had. Which is why I guess I could no longer focus on the woman in front of me since I had spotted Starr on ground level.

"I'm sorry, but I need to go." I handed her a pamphlet and barely looked at her as I made my way over to the gate that separated the parade participants from spectators.

I walked towards her the same way I made my way over to her that night in the club, except this time she didn't beckon me over with a crooked finger. This time, I knew it was my proper position to approach her. I just didn't know exactly how the conversation would pan out given how things went between us the last time I had seen her.

And as the morning sun hit my exposed legs and arms since I had a Black Panther tank top and cargo shorts on, I found myself being that guy. The one that studied a woman's curves to a fault. But damn, how could I not be that guy? How could I not admire, ogle the way her deep rich melanin popped against the big feathers and shiny material of her orange and yellow costume. A black woman in orange or yellow was my weakness, but the combo against her skin? It, she was a sight to behold and I had to shift my messenger bag in front of me. I didn't want to approach her with a visible hard-on, a telling sign of one of the effects she had on me.

Our eyes remained locked with one another and my stride slowed down as I made my way across the grass and over to her.

The longer I stared at her, standing there and allowing me to take her in, the more I realized she was a total package, a dream woman of sorts. Every encounter I had with her showcased how educated and woke she was.

Her standing in her career told the bold tale of how ambitious she was, a top trait that had to be evident in a woman I wanted to pursue. And sexy? That went without saying, but it wasn't because she was in front of me with barely any clothes on since the feathers sprouting out like wings on her back were far bigger than the small, triangular patches of fabric covering her beautiful breasts and crotch. My eyes traveled down to those thick thighs of hers that I loved. But even they didn't tip her scales for me. She was sexy because of the confidence she exuded and the passion she spoke with every time she opened her mouth.

I made it up to the short, makeshift gate and stopped in front of her. "Starr."

"Christopher."

"Oh, so this is him." A full-figured, medium brown-skinned woman in a similar costume as Starr's drew closer to Starr. The woman turned her full attention to me. "Christopher, why do you keep giving my girl a hard time?"

"Hunh?" My forehead scrunched as I stared at the stranger and then at Starr, who was shaking her head and mumbling something to the stranger who seemed to be her friend.

"I'm just saying, I don't know you, but from the way Starr describes her encounters with you and the way I saw you grinding on her that night at the club, you like her. You're obviously just too stubborn, too prideful to admit it. This is a good one here." She pointed at Starr. "Get out your little feelings because my girl is driving in her own lane and is not willing to jump out her car, get into yours and let you drive her to your destination."

"Rikia, would you please take her over there somewhere?" Starr sighed and pointed in the direction of a crowd of men and women dressed in the same colored costumes as her and her two friends.

"Gladly," Rikia said and pushed the other resistant and giggling friend away from us.

Starr waited until they were out of earshot and then turned back to face me. "I am so sorry for that."

"No need to be. They say a drunk mouth speaks a sober mind."

"But she wasn't drunk, that's how she is on the regular."

I could only laugh at that and soon, the beautiful sound of Starr's laughter met my ears.

"Duly noted. And her sober mind and mouth

were right." I couldn't help but smile at her raised eyebrows and slightly gaped mouth.

"Is that an apology?"

"No, that's the intro to one," I said.

"Oh," she said, somewhat still shocked. The unassuming expression on her face endeared her to me all the more.

"Your friend was right. I was wrong for suggesting that my interests were greater than yours and that you should abandon your cause to help push mine. For that, I apologize."

"Well Christopher, how becoming of you. I accept your apology."

"Thank you. I'm happy to hear that because truth is, had I listened to you more so than what I had, I would have gotten your plight beyond the superficial level I made it out to be."

"I don't follow."

"Not sure if you remember since I was talking sideways when I came to your class that day—"

"Indeed, you were." She smiled and her seemingly forgiveness of how big of a jerk I had been to her at times confirmed to me just how awesome of a woman she was.

"I hadn't even watched your full segment on Windy City Live, because had I, I would've learned how you recently found out about your Jamaican roots and how it was the catalyst to send you on your journey to bring the Carnivale to Chicago."

She nodded.

"I know I don't even deserve for you to hear me out, but when I watched the clip, I could hear the passion in your voice for your newly found ancestry. And if I can be completely honest without being judged?"

"Oh, please do." She pursed her lips and stared at me with a glint of humor in her eyes.

"But, but—' I held my hands up to provide additional support for me. "In my defense, this is the day and age of social media, so if a person puts their life on the different platforms, they shouldn't expect privacy and in fact, welcome people into their business."

"True." She nodded her head.

"Well, I came across your article or maybe it was a journal entry, since it seemed so intimate and raw, where you recounted your trip to Jamaica, how you met your aunt, found out who your father was, and your journey into the dig thereafter. It was moving. You are moving. When you speak about your passions and lecture your class, you remind me of me."

She cocked her head and I could only laugh. "Okay, a better me."

"You're not all that bad." She stepped closer to the gate and it seemed like an invite for me to do so as well, so I closed more of the space between us.

"Thanks. I'm not sure what inspired you to be a

black studies professor, something I'd like to get to know if you'd let me, but whether I know the reason or not yet, I see your passion for it and it takes me back to why I became so passionate about the African American plight in our communities."

She smiled that pretty, high wattage smile of hers and said, "Since you at least know what motivated me to spearhead getting the Carnivale here, what has you so on go for *us*?"

"In short, my dad was a Black Panther."

Her eyes lit up with a pride and a sense of awe that I always imagined my future wife's face would have when I told her about my origins. I wanted a wife with pride like hers to be by my side when I shared with our future kids the stories my father told me of all he'd gone through as a Panther.

I simply appreciated the attention she was giving me and my story. I enjoyed looking into her eyes and taking in the peaceful space we existed in at the moment. So much so that I didn't want to cut through the energy with words, but I equally wanted to share more of my past with her as a means to bind us closer together. "Given what you do for a living, I'm certain you know all about the Party and what they stood for."

"That is correct."

"So there's no need to give you their background and what they did for us back then and for generations to come, but seeing my dad take pride in what he stood for as a member, it always made me want to be just like him. Continue his legacy of uplifting and protecting the black community in Chicago. It's what drives me to physically train as many clients as I can early in the day and then get over to the alderman's office to educate and host the meetings that I do for the rest of my day."

"And all that you do is very admirable. So am I right to assume that the 'beef' between us has been cooked?"

"Funny spin on that cliché." I laughed as I pointed at her. "And yes, I can't be beefing with the woman I want to get to know more. You down for that?"

"Good, because since I'm down to get to know you more, I'mma need you to see that this Carnivale was necessary, is a beautiful thing, and does not take away or diminish your fight."

I bit my bottom lip and didn't bother to hide the wide smile covering most of my face as I stared at her. "I can't argue with that. Especially since there are some faces here I haven't seen before. Just means there are new people here to pass my pamphlets out to." I shook the stack I had been holding in my hand the entire time I had been talking to her.

She giggled. "You can look at it that way, but I'd rather you just try and enjoy the weekend with me." She shimmied and my eyes traveled up and down a body that I knew smelled good and felt so good against mine. "I was suggesting that you enjoy the Carnivale festivities and play mas', participate in it, and not just enjoy looking at me." She giggled and pulled me out of the vivid and suddenly dirty thoughts of us together.

"I'm sorry for just staring at you and I hope that it didn't creep you out, but do you know how fine you are? Not just because you barely have anything on, but everything about you screams, 'I'm the ish'."

"My looks say that, hunh?" The cute lilt in her voice and the soft grin on her face made me laugh.

"Yes...can I?" I reached out just short of her wild hair.

"Sure." She tilted her head towards my hand and twisted the ends of a tight coil around my finger as she brought her eyes back up to look into mine. "So you like my hair as much as I like yours?"

Her voice was dipped in just enough sugar to hit the spot. She had a subtle way of flirting with me that I couldn't wait to get more of.

"Yeah, I do. It makes me think you're a free spirit and in touch with and not ashamed of your roots."

"Yeah, yours makes me think that you don't conform to societal norms that suggest how we should look, but enough about hair. How about you come on this side of the fence and enjoy the band and parades with me since we're allies now?"

"Allies?" I laughed.

"Yes, or is that not what the apology was for?" She feigned being offended.

"Nah, you're right. We're allies, but I'm hoping to make us be more than just allies. And with the little I know about participating in these kinds of things, I can't just be over there with y'all in my black tank and cargo shorts."

She put her pointer finger up to her mouth as if she were seriously contemplating something, but I knew she was being dramatic when a smile cracked her pretty face and she said, "Well, you have the body to ditch the shirt and your cargo shorts do kind of blend in with our orange and yellow."

"You're reaching." I laughed and she joined in with me.

"I am. I'm reaching out for you to hop the fence and play mas' with me. I know for a fact that the costume designers for my band made a few extras for men and women. She's under that tent." She pointed to a big white tent to the right of her. "Although fairly expensive, I wholeheartedly believe that you would enjoy yourself with us, with me."

"Well, when you put it like that, how can I say no?" I hopped the fence, bought one of the additional costumes, and rushed into one of the porta potties to change my clothes.

In no time, I was in orange shorts, a yellow and orange shoulder harness of some sort that draped a string down the middle of my chest and a big, feathered headpiece of all things on my head. "So, how do I look?" I spread my arms wide as I walked towards a smiling Starr.

"I don't think it'd be proper to put into words how you really look to me at this time." She winked and I chuckled, learning that she was just as pleased with how I looked in my costume as I thought she was in hers. "Simply put, you look...scrumptious. That shea butter with SPF she handed you before you went into that stall really highlights your muscle definition. You look like a god of some sort."

I closed the distance between us and the heat from the high sun beating on my bare back had nothing on the heat from the fire burning between us.

When a long string of quiet yet engaging and telling silence passed between us, her sweet voice rose above our muted conversation. "Come on." She locked her hand in mine and began to sway her body in tandem with the soca music booming around us and said, "Let's go play mas together on this concrete island you and I love so much. Chicago."

Epilogue

Starr

4 Months Later

"Insert the card into the machine. And congratulations for voting for your first time ever." I pointed to the machine in front of me.

The eighteen-year-old nodded his head at me with a dumbfounded look on his face.

"He had no choice. I told him that it was his civic duty. He had to help this country crawl out of the hell hole morons put it in four years ago when they voted that fool in office." The young man's father spoke up for his son.

The father's words were like an echo of most of the people who had come in to vote that day and once again, I had to keep my lips pressed tightly and not laugh as loud and as hard as I had wanted to. I was a volunteer and was supposed to be impartial as I helped the voters at the polls.

The father and son combo left, and Chris began speaking to us all. "Well, that was the last voters for the night. You all showed up and helped tremendously for our local elections last year and you definitely showed up for our presidential election today.

"Be proud of the work you do to make your voices, our voices heard. We're gaining ground with making people aware of the black exodus from Chicago and we've even gotten City Hall to take us more seriously on the matter.

"We're working with them to begin to implement some of the things I outlined in my plan. Things are not moving as fast as I'd like them to, but they're moving. We can make change when we work together." Chris looked at me with the last of his words and I swear I couldn't wait until we got back to his place or mine to show him just how much he turned me on when he was on his whole "community activist, I'mma save my people" ish.

But in the meantime, I was left to simply admire the man who had easily become my man once we got past our sordid moments and embraced the fact that we can accomplish more together than apart.

I smiled as I watched him shake a few hands before he turned to me and helped me put my coat on since it was November and rather chilly outside. When my peacoat was buttoned up, I looked up at him and said, "You know, a lot of people wrote you in on the ballot. Maybe you should consider running to hold an office and affect change that way."

One of his thick brows lifted as his hand raised and he laid the back of it on my forehead.

I giggled and pushed his hand away from me. "I don't have a fever, silly."

"You must be feverish to suggest something like that to me. What have we been talking about these past four months we've been together if you think that I would ever want a career in politics?"

"We know each other quite well, wouldn't you agree?" My voice lowered as I leaned in and pressed my lips against his.

"Mmmhh." He held me tightly in his arms but pulled back from my kiss and said, "If only Mrs. Rutledge wasn't around that corner with DeMarcus, I would take you in the back and remind you of just how much we're acquainted with each other. Have you screaming out all the patois words you know." He bit my earlobe and squeezed my butt, causing me to giggle and squirm in his arms.

"You are so silly, but I can't wait to get back to your place so you can make good on your promise." I winked and bit my bottom lip as I pulled away from his embrace that I had come to enjoy being in.

"Bet. And just so we're clear, Chicago politics

are so corrupt that I would never try to be a politician." He sighed. "I know being one would change me and not for the better."

"Why, you think it would question your integrity to the point that you'd lose it?"

"Nah, I would never let it make me less of a man. That's why I wouldn't become one. They all end up compromising in ways that are unhealthily foreign to them. But being one would make me grumpier than I was when I first met you."

"And we definitely can't have that." I laughed as I dodged his grasp that I knew would've led to him tickling my sides until I begged him for mercy to let up on me.

"Don't worry. I'll touch you all over when we get back to my place." He warned me with a look of mischief in his eyes. "And I'm fine with the position that I have now. I like the pressure I can apply as an activist. Besides, I know I wouldn't be able to enjoy this concrete island of ours as a politician. Come on, let's go so I can explore the lush island that is your body."

ALSO BY ANITA DAVIS

Sisterhood Chronicles Series
Underneath It All
Discovery
Untold
When It Happens To You
All Things Considered

Forever Friends Series
Catch Me If You Can
It's Complicated

Limelight Series
Hues
Tones
Vision

Love Alive Series
The Kissing Game

Concord Ave Shorts
On the House

Standalone Titles
After All Is Said & Done
The Bid Catcher: Distinguished Gentlemen Series

*(Best if you read Forever Friends series before
reading Sisterhood Chronicles 3)*

ABOUT THE AUTHOR

Anita Davis is a former elementary teacher born and raised in Chicago. Although she wrote short stories much of her childhood, she didn't unlock and cultivate her passion as a writer until she became a writing teacher for middle school students. The more she had to create sample writings for her students, the more she realized her passion and ability to tell stories in the written form. She decided to hone her craft as a writer by completing her Master of Fine Arts in Creative Writing via National University. She now pursues writing books most of her time, in addition to being a flight attendant. Anita seeks to encourage, engage, and entertain her readers.

She is Co-Founder of Book Euphoria, a group of Chicago authors bound by their love of literature. Book Euphoria hosts literary events and they also founded the empowerment movement, Black Girl Passion.

Anita writes contemporary romantic women's fiction and seeks to encourage, engage, and entertain her readers.

authoranitadavis@gmail.com
www.authoranitadavis.com
Facebook: Anita Davis and Author page: Author Anita Davis
Instagram: @authoranitadavis   Twitter: @_AnitaDavis